SUPER-SAVER MOUSE

Sandi Toksvig

Illustrated by
George Hollingworth

CORGI PUPS

For Jesse, Megan and Ted – S.T.

SUPER-SAVER MOUSE
A CORGI PUPS BOOK

First publication in Great Britain

PRINTING HISTORY
Corgi Pups edition published 1999

ISBN 0 552 54940 1

Set in 18/25pt Bembo Schoolbook by
Phoenix Typesetting, Ilkley, West Yorkshire

Corgi Pups Books are published by Transworld Publishers,
61-63 Uxbridge Road, Ealing, London W5 5SA,
a division of the Random House Group Ltd,
in Australia by Random House Australia (Pty) Ltd,
20 Alfred Street, Milsons Point, Sydney, NSW 2061, Australia
in New Zealand by Random House New Zealand Ltd,
18 Poland Road, Glenfield, Auckland 10, New Zealand
and in South Africa by Random House (Pty) Ltd,
Endulini, 5a Jubilee Road, Parktown 2193, South Africa

Printed and bound in Denmark by
Nørhaven Paperback, Viborg

Contents

Series reading consultant: Prue Goodwin,
Reading and Language Information Centre,
University of Reading

Chapter One

Boris was a tube mouse. He lived in the tube. Not in a tube of sweets. He had tried living in a tube of sweets and it was not at all comfortable. No, Boris lived in the tube in London.

The tube is what people in London call the underground railway. A lot of mice live in the tube. If you look carefully you can see them scurrying about in the tunnels and under the raised train tracks. Tube mice are tiny but they eat a lot. This is not a

Danger

problem because there is plenty
of food. People are always
dropping a bit of bread roll here
or a scrap of chocolate there. It
may look like rubbish to some
but it is a three-course dinner to
a little mouse.

The tube is made up of lots of different railway lines all criss-crossing under the city. Boris learned about it from his great-great-great-great-great-great-grandfather Garibaldi. He lived in an old biscuit packet on the Bakerloo Line and knew everything.

"It's called the tube," explained Grandfather Garibaldi, "because trains go all over London in giant tubes under the ground. They go to famous places like Piccadilly Circus and Leicester Square and even to places you've never heard of like Cricklewood."

Boris lived in Camden Town station. For a little mouse he was very bright and curious. From the day he was born he was interested in everything.

"Baker Street was the first tube station ever built," Grandfather Garibaldi told him when Boris was still a tiny, very pink mouse.

"The very first?" squeaked Boris.

"Yes," said Garibaldi, nibbling on half a cheddar cheese sandwich which had been dropped by a man in a hurry.

"I bet no-one used it," said
Boris thoughtfully.

"Why?" asked his
grandfather.

"Well, if it was the *first* tube
station then there would be
nowhere for people to go. They

would have to wait for the
second one to open."

Grandfather Garibaldi
nodded, chortling to himself. The
tube was always so busy he had
never thought about it not being
full of people. Little Boris had a
good brain but even Grandfather
didn't yet know how good.

Chapter Two

Boris had a cousin called Kicker.
It is an unusual name for a
mouse but mice have a lot of
children and they run out of
names. Kicker's mum had had
142 children the year he was

born. Kicker was number 141
and his mum couldn't think
what to call him. She saw the
word "Kicker" on the side of
someone's shoe and thought it
would do for her son.

Boris liked Kicker because he
was so cool. He swaggered when
he walked, which is quite a
trick for a mouse.

Kicker was daring too. Once he had tried nibbling on a cigarette end he and Boris had found near the ticket office. He knew he wasn't supposed to, and it made him sick, but that was what Kicker was like.

"When I grow up, I'm going to live somewhere famous like Marble Arch or Hyde Park Corner. I shall ride the trains and sometimes I might even go out of the station," boasted Kicker.

Boris laughed. Mice never went on to trains but he liked the idea.

Besides Kicker, Boris had one other good friend. His name was Heavy Duty and he was a human, not at all the usual sort of chum for a tube mouse.

Heavy Duty was a very small, very thin man who cleaned the station every morning before the passengers arrived.

He had a big wide broom and a
dustpan and he went up and
down the platform sweeping up
anything the mice hadn't
wanted for dinner. One
morning, when Boris was very
small, Heavy Duty had swept
him up and put him in the
dustpan.

Boris was just falling into a
black bag of rubbish when
Heavy Duty caught him in his
hand.

"Hello, little fellow," he said.
Boris was not at all sure
whether humans ate mice so he
shut his eyes and shook all over.

"Sssh," said Heavy Duty,
stroking Boris's head with his

enormous hand. "You're all
right." Heavy Duty fished about
in the front pocket of his overalls
and pulled out a chocolate
biscuit. He put Boris back on the
platform and crumbled the
biscuit next to him. Boris was in
mouse heaven.

Then some boys turned up.
They were waiting for a train
and they started teasing Heavy
Duty. Heavy Duty just kept on
sweeping until one of them
stepped in front of the big
broom.

"Hey, you," said the rough boy, pushing Heavy Duty. "Are you a man or a mouse?" His friends all laughed. Heavy Duty didn't say a word but it made Boris mad. He wished he was big enough to help his new friend.

After that, Boris used to get up early every morning, before any of the other mice thought it was worth it, and play with old Heavy Duty.

One Monday, about half an hour before the first train was due, Boris scampered out onto the southbound platform to play with Heavy Duty. The platform was empty. There was no sign of Heavy Duty. This was very odd.

Boris checked
the northbound
platform. Still
nothing.
Boris went
back to the
southbound platform and at the
far end he saw Heavy Duty's
broom and dustpan lying on the
ground.

Although he felt scared,
something made Boris peep over
the edge of the platform and
onto the track. To his horror,

24

there lying across the tracks was
Heavy Duty. He had obviously
fallen and didn't look as if he
could get up. His eyes were still
open and he looked straight up
at Boris on the platform.

"Help!" moaned Heavy Duty.

"Help?" repeated Boris. "Help! Oh, I must get help." Boris wasn't at all sure where to begin. He ran to get Kicker.

"Kicker, Kicker, wake up!" cried Boris, as he ran towards the old film box which Kicker called home. "There's been an accident!"

Boris dragged his half-awake cousin onto the platform. Kicker shook his head as Boris pulled him to the edge to look down at Heavy Duty on the track.

"Help," groaned Heavy Duty.

"He needs help," said Kicker confidently.

"I know that!" shouted Boris. "That's why I got you."

"Right," said Kicker, squaring his shoulders and trying to look as if he was just the mouse for the job. "We need to help." Kicker looked over the edge of the platform one more time.

"Uh, Boris, he's quite big. Not that I can't manage but, I mean, compared to us . . ."

Suddenly Boris went as pale as it is possible for a small mouse who has never had any sun to go. "Kicker! The train! Heavy Duty is right in the way. We've got to stop the first train!"

Chapter Three

Boris had seen trains come and go all his life. He knew what they could do to things left on the line. He also knew they came from the big tunnel at the end of the platform. Without thinking, he jumped down to the ground under the track and began to run towards the darkness. "Come on, Kicker," he called as he ran.

Kicker swallowed hard. All his life he had talked about leaving the station but he hadn't thought it would be like this. Not this quick. Not without packing or saying goodbye to his mum, but he couldn't let Boris think he was scared. Boris was nearly at the tunnel when Kicker jumped down after him. The two mice sped into the dark space.

It was much darker in the tunnel than on the platform and it took them a while to adjust to the light as they ran. They had not gone more than a minute when Boris suddenly screeched to a halt.

"Can't stop, can't stop!" yelled Kicker, crashing into his cousin.

"What are you doing?" he asked irritably, standing on his head.

"The tunnel," panted Boris. "It splits in two. I don't know which way the train will come."

Kicker looked around. The track went off in two different

directions. Neither young mouse
had ever been in the tunnel
before and they had no idea
which way to go.

"Now what?" groaned Kicker.

"Grandfather Garibaldi!" shouted Boris, running back the way they had come.

Garibaldi was just having his morning wash when the two young mice burst into his biscuit packet.

"Do you mind?" he said in his crossest voice.

"Grandfather, Grandfather, where does the first train come from?" panted Boris.

Grandfather took this as a different sort of question. He stopped to think for a minute. "It depends what you believe. There are different theories . . ."

"No," said Boris, "the timetable. What time is the first train of the morning?"

"Six o'clock," replied the confused old mouse.

"And where does it come from?" persisted Boris.

Garibaldi stopped to think for a moment. "Edgware. I went there once, you know. Used to know a very pretty little mouse in . . ."

"Is that right or left where the tunnel splits?" shouted Kicker, knowing they didn't have time for one of Garibaldi's stories.

"Oh, let's see. Left, I think. Yes, that would be left."

Kicker and Boris ran off
leaving Garibaldi to shake his
head over the manners of young
mice.

The two small tube mice ran
back down the tunnel into the
dark. When the tunnel split in
two they didn't hesitate but ran

along the left side as fast as
they could. Soon they reached
the station where the trains stop
before they get to Camden
Town. Kicker and Boris leant
against the tunnel wall
breathing hard.

"No train yet," wheezed
Boris.

"No," said Kicker, coughing from the running.

Boris looked up at the sign on the platform. The letters were huge. "CHALK FARM" it read. There were already people on the platform waiting for the first train.

"We've still got time to stop it," said Boris.

"Yes," said Kicker and then paused. He asked the question Boris hadn't wanted to think about. "How will we do that?"

Boris didn't get a chance to answer. Before he could speak a terrible noise began bellowing from the other end of the platform. Bright lights swung out of a dark tunnel and swept towards the mice.

Chapter Four

Kicker forgot entirely about
being cool.

"Aaargh!" he shrieked and
tried to hide behind Boris. The
train came closer and closer
until Kicker couldn't stand it for

another
minute. He
ran off
squeaking,
back the
way they had come. Boris was
alone. The train came to a halt
about a metre away and Boris
looked up at it. It was the
biggest thing he had ever seen.

"This is ridiculous," he said
to himself. "I'm much too little
and . . ." Then he remembered
his friend Heavy Duty and he
knew he had to do something.

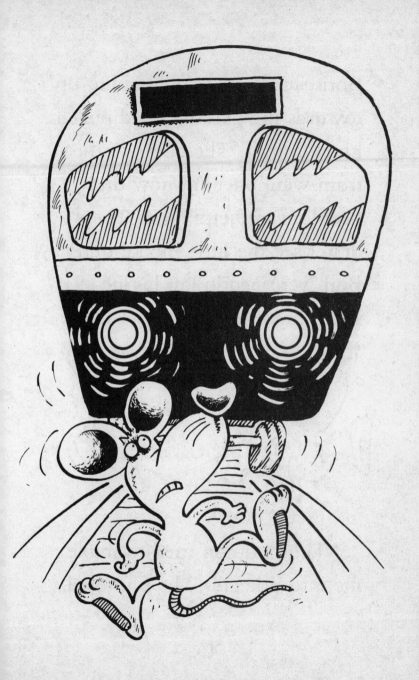

Boris spied some cable going up towards the platform and pulled himself up it. The doors of the train were opening now and people were getting on. They didn't see the little mouse and Boris very nearly lost his life to a sharp high heel.

"That woman tried to make me into a kebab," he muttered,

but no-one could hear him. No-one was looking for a mouse on the tube at that time of the morning. Boris looked around for some emergency cable he could chew through or an alarm he could set off but there didn't seem to be any. Then an announcement boomed across the platform.

"Mind the gap," said a loud voice. It made Boris jump.

He was feeling very nervous. He had never been to another station before and this one seemed extremely busy.

"It's just an announcement," he said to himself, trying to calm down. "To say the train is leaving." Suddenly Boris realized what that meant. "The train is

 leaving!" he shrieked. Before he had time to think, Boris did

48

something his mother had told
him never to do. He jumped
from the platform onto the train
just as the doors were closing.

He didn't know whether it was
brave or foolish.

Chapter Five

None of the passengers saw
Boris. They were all much too
busy reading their newspapers
and trying not to look at each
other. Boris tried to decide what
to do. From behind a large pair

of trainers he could
see a lot of signs
high above his

EMERGENCY
STOP

head. There were different
pictures of people washing their
hair, taking trips and smiling in
banks. None of that was helpful
but then he saw something that
was. A red handle with the words
"EMERGENCY STOP" on it.
It was perfect. This was an
emergency and
he needed the
train to stop. The
only problem was
reaching it.

Boris knew time was
running out. He saw
a woman standing
near the handle.
She was very tall
and wore a large
black coat with a
matching hat
covered in fruit
and flowers.
Next to
her was a
tall
shopping
bag full
of food.

If Boris could get up to the apple on her hat then he could probably reach the emergency handle. Starting at her shopping bag, he began to climb.

Now climbing a shopping bag for you and me might be nothing but to a mouse it was like a mountain. Boris climbed and climbed. Up to the handles,

over some sticks of
bread, onto the
woman's coat
and up
towards the hat.

He climbed as quietly as
possible, past the woman's sleeve
and onto her collar. As Boris
reached the hat he knew he

would have to be quick. He
could feel the train beginning to
slow down. People were starting
to shuffle their things together to
get off. Boris had just reached
the apple on the hat and was
stretching out his tiny body to
haul down the emergency
handle when . . .

EMERGENCY
STOP

a man opposite did something
very unusual on a tube train. He
spoke.

"I say," he said to the woman Boris had just climbed up, "there's a mouse in your hat."

He might as well have said she was on fire. He would have got the same reaction. The woman instantly screamed. She grabbed her hat and pulled it from her head. Boris flew out across the carriage and landed in the lap of a man reading *The Times*.

He jumped up, shook his paper and catapulted Boris two seats along to a woman holding a pot plant. Boris landed in a jungle of leaves and looked up to see ten people all shrieking at him.

"Heavy Duty is on the track," he shrieked back, but the humans had no idea what he was saying. It just sounded like squeaks to them and that made the pot-plant woman go mad. She dropped her plant and just when Boris thought all was lost, she reached up and pulled the emergency handle.

Chapter Six

The train stopped just half a
metre away from Heavy Duty.
In all the confusion Boris
managed to slip away when the
doors opened. Underground staff
were running everywhere.
Someone called out that she was

a doctor and began to help
Heavy Duty. Everyone was
talking.

"Poor man must have tripped over the edge."

"How dreadful."

"Is he all right?" asked the man who had been reading *The Times*. The doctor assured everyone that Heavy Duty would be just fine. Everyone tried to be helpful except the pot-plant woman from the train. She was useless. She just kept screaming, "What about the mouse! A mouse!"

"What an incredible piece of luck, the train stopping like that," said all the people after Heavy Duty had been saved. No-one knew it was Boris who had done the saving.

Grandfather Garibaldi said that was typical. A tube mouse did a public service and no-one gave him credit. Kicker told

everyone about his trip to Chalk
Farm but he forgot to mention
the part about running away.

Heavy Duty knew who had
saved him. About a week later
he and Boris were playing with
the broom when the rough boys
came back. They headed
towards Heavy Duty, ready to
tease him.

"Before you ask again if I am a man or a mouse," Heavy Duty said loudly, stopping them in their tracks, "I've decided. I would much rather be a mouse. A brave mouse." Heavy Duty

winked at Boris and he wasn't the least bit surprised to see Boris wink back.

THE END